For my sister Heidi
S. F.

For Sam and Ben
K. B. R.

Text copyright © 2007 by Susan Fletcher
Illustrations copyright © 2007 by Kimberly Bulcken Root

First edition 2007

Library of Congress Cataloging-in-Publication Data is available.
Library of Congress Card Number 2006051833
ISBN 978-0-7636-2263-3

2 4 6 8 10 9 7 5 3 1

Printed in Singapore

This book was typeset in Egyptian Extended.
The illustrations were done in pencil and watercolor.

Candlewick Press
2067 Massachusetts Avenue
Cambridge, Massachusetts 02140

visit us at www.candlewick.com

DADBLAMED
UNION ARMY
COW

SUSAN FLETCHER

illustrated by
KIMBERLY BULCKEN
ROOT

CANDLEWICK PRESS
CAMBRIDGE, MASSACHUSETTS

That dadblamed cow!
When I went to join
the Union Army,
she did not stay home
like a regular cow
but followed me down
to the enlistment office.
"You git on home,
you dadblamed cow,"
I told her.

Dadblamed cow said,
"Moo."

That dadblamed cow!
When I went off
to the railway station
to ride with my regiment,
I told her,
"Git home now,
you dadblamed cow."
But she snuck onboard
when nobody was looking.
"Whose dadblamed cow is this?"
Captain asked.

Dadblamed cow said,
"Moo."

That dadblamed cow!
She followed me to the war.

Marched step by step
all the way South.
Clop two three four,
Clop two three four.
Dadblamed, footsore cow!

When my army buddies
were whittlin'
or playin' cards
or takin' a snooze,
I had to hunt all over creation
for a mess of unstomped grass.
"You're a dadblamed
    persnickety cow,"
I said.

When she got mired
in knee-high mud,
took three of us in front
and four behind—
sweat-soaked,
rope-burned,
hoof-bruised—
to haul her out.
"You're a dadblamed *heavy* cow,"
I said.

When bullets went whistlin'
past our ears,
she got spooked and bolted—
around a clump of cannon,
through a bramble patch,
over a hill,
across a creek,
and right smack-dab
into a pack of horse dragoons.
"You're a dadblamed
    dangerous cow," I said.

But . . .

when flies buzzed 'round our heads
on summer days,
she come in mighty useful.

When frost nipped our toes
in the middle of the night,
she come in mighty useful.

When food got scarce
late in the war,
she come in mighty useful.

"Good thing you brought
that dadblamed cow,"
Captain said.

Dadblamed cow said,
"Moo."

I took a musket ball
in my shoulder.
Missed my heart by just that much.
That cow followed me down
to the army hospital.
"You git on back,
you dadblamed cow!" I told her.
"They need you now,
you dadblamed cow."

Dadblamed cow said,
"Moo."

Doc Henry says
milk built up my strength.
Mine, and a peck of others' too.
That dadblamed cow!
She wouldn't budge from my bedside,
even for unstomped grass.

When the war done ended,
she followed me home.
Limped step by step
all the way North.
Clop . . . two . . . three . . . four.
Clop . . . two . . . three . . . four.
Tired old dadblamed cow.

A newspaper reporter
heard about me
(and that dadblamed cow).
He took some pictures,
questioned me some
'bout what we did in the war.

But when that paper come out,
only one of us was in it:

dotty old dadblamed cow!

Now folks come from miles around
to scratch between her horns,
to feed her their best clover,
to moon right into her eyes.

Pa and me built her
a brand-new shed,
purtier than our house!

Captain come by with a medal—
all shiny-bright
with a blue-and-red stripy ribbon
For brave and unusual
service to country
is writ right there on the back.

"You're a dadblamed hero now," I told her.
"Plain old hay ain't sweet enough.
 Saggy old shed ain't fine enough.
 Reckon you're too all–fired
 high–and–mighty
 to even *talk* to the likes of me."

That dadblamed cow said . . .

A NOTE FROM THE AUTHOR

This book is based on a true story about a cow that marched with the Union Army during the Civil War. I heard the tale from Linda Thompson, media specialist at Zellerbach Elementary School in Camas, Washington. Linda first learned about the Union Army cow from her grandfather's cousin, Mrs. H. F. Rethers, the daughter of Captain Jesse M. Lee, the captain of the regiment to which the cow was attached.

I have taken liberties with history, as fiction writers are wont to do. However, this much is corroborated by newspaper clippings, photographs, and Mrs. Rethers: From 1862 to 1865, a "celebrated cow" traveled with the Fifty-Ninth Regiment of Indiana Volunteers, giving milk to the soldiers. She was in the Vicksburg and Atlanta campaigns; she traveled through the Carolinas and Virginia to Washington City, where she passed in review with the army. She is said to have traveled many hundreds of miles and witnessed a hundred engagements and skirmishes. The milk may well have saved the soldiers' lives, as the supply train couldn't keep up with them and, as Mrs. Rethers has written, "hardtack and wormy bacon weren't very nourishing." Captain Lee mustered out at six feet two inches, weighing 110 pounds.

After the war, the cow was written up in the Greencastle, Indiana, newspaper. She spent her days contentedly in the pasture of Professor George Lee (Captain Jesse Lee's brother) until she died many years later.